"Hello!"
said Tallulah.

THIS
WAY UP

I ♥ 🐱

"Miaow?"
said the ears.

But Tallulah knew **exactly** what to do to make Tom feel at home.

She put a tiny saucer of milk outside his box and waited . . . and waited.

Soon she was showing him all around the house.

When Tom met Tallulah

Rosie Reeve

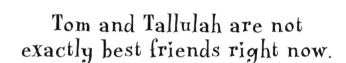

Tom and Tallulah are not
exactly best friends right now.

Find out why inside . . .

BLOOMSBURY

LONDON   NEW DELHI   NEW YORK   SYDNEY

AKIRK

When Tom met Tallulah he was **extremely** shy – too shy to even come out of his box.

He was just a pair of furry ears.

She even drew a map so he could find all the best places for cat-napping.

It was a Cat-nap Map.

Tallulah showed Tom his very own back door.

She even made him
a special toy.

Tom was amazed at how well Tallulah understood **cat**.
She seemed to know exactly what he wanted
from a simple **purr** or a **miaow**.

In no time at all, Tom had settled into his new home perfectly.

Tom decided that since Tallulah seemed to be so good at **cat**, he should try to learn **human**.

But he didn't tell anyone.

He just secretly followed Tallulah around
and took notes in his little black book.

One morning, Tom got up
and went to the bathroom.

He brushed his teeth
and combed his whiskers.

Then he got dressed . . .

and had breakfast.

By the time Tallulah came downstairs,
Tom had already made her
a special toy to play with.

But whilst Tom seemed to be getting
better and better at **human**,
Tallulah's **cat** was not improving **at all**.

She got in a tangle with the string.

ouch!

She spilt her milk.

oops!

She got stuck in the door.

z z z z z z z z z z

And she cat-napped in all
the **wrong** places!

But Tom remembered how patient
Tallulah had been with him.

So he waited . . . and waited . . .

Before long, Tallulah began
to settle into things nicely.

At bedtime, Tom laid his clothes
neatly on the bed.

Tallulah purred sleepily.

And that was when Tom knew
that the time was right.

The next morning, Tom got up early
and went to the pet shop.

"She's beautifully house-trained," he said.
"She'll make a lovely pet for somebody.

But could I exchange her . . ."

"For a **puppy**?"

Oops! **Someone** has not been very nice . . .

To Charles, Vicky, Patrick and Iona ~ RR

Bloomsbury Publishing, London, New Delhi, New York and Sydney

First published in Great Britain in 2013 by Bloomsbury Publishing Plc
50 Bedford Square, London, WC1B 3DP

Text and Illustrations copyright © Rosie Reeve 2013
The moral rights of the author/illustrator have been asserted

A CIP catalogue record for this book is available from the British Library

ISBN 978 1 4088 3698 9 (HB)
ISBN 978 1 4088 3699 6 (PB)
ISBN 978 1 4088 3963 8 (eBook)

FSC
www.fsc.org

MIX
Paper from
responsible sources
FSC® C008047

Printed in China by C & C Offset Printing Co Ltd, Shenzhen, Guangdong

1 3 5 7 9 10 8 6 4 2